MAXFIELD PARRISH

A TREASURY
of ART
and CHILDREN'S
LITERATURE

MAXFIELD PARRISH

A TREASURY
of ART
and CHILDREN'S
LITERATURE

COMPILED BY

ALMA GILBERT

ILLUSTRATED BY

MAXFIELD PARRISH

ATHENEUM BOOKS for YOUNG READERS

Atheneum Books for Young Readers
An imprint of Simon & Schuster Children's Publishing Division
1230 Avenue of the Americas
New York, NY 10020

Designed by Virginia Pope

The text of this book is set in Perpetua

First edition

Printed in Mexico

10 9 8 7 6 5 4 3 2 1

Library of Congress Catalog Card Number: 95-060385

ISBN: 0-689-80300-1

ACKNOWLEDGMENTS

The author gratefully acknowledges the loan of transparencies of Parrish illustrations by owners of the originals or owners of transparencies not in the author's collection, particularly: The Detroit Institute of Arts, Detroit, Michigan; Pennsylvania Academy of the Fine Arts, Philadelphia, Pennsylvania; The Charles Hosmer Morse Museum of American Art, Winter Park, Florida; and The Fine Arts Museums of San Francisco, San Francisco, California.

The author also gratefully acknowledges the suggestions and advice given in the preparation and format of this book by Phil Wood, Veronica Randall, David Charlsen and Jackie Wan of Tenspeed Publications, and the legal advice on this and other literary matters offered by Anthony Diepenbrock of Townsend and Townsend, Khourie and Crew.

CONTENTS

Backward, turn backward, O Time in your flight!
Make me a child again, just for to-night!...
Backward, flow backward, O tide of the years!
I am so weary of toils and of tears,
Toil without recompense, tears all in vain!
Take them, and give me my childhood again...

—From "Rock Me to Sleep" by Elizabeth Akers Allen
(1832–1911)

MAXFIELD PARRISH

(1870-1966)

Every hundred years or so, we find an artist whose talent and art make a statement that leaves an indelible mark on the consciousness of the generations who come in contact with his or her work. Maxfield Parrish was such an artist. It is fitting that in 1995, the 125th anniversary of his birth and the hundredth anniversary of his first published work, his images and illustrations are still being sought after and enjoyed by a multitude of international collectors.

Fred Maxfield Parrish (M. P. to his family, friends, and close associates) was born July 25, 1870, in Philadelphia to Stephen Parrish, a well-known artist and etcher, and his wife, Elizabeth Bancroft Parrish. Maxfield was a descendant of generations of beloved Philadelphia Quaker physicians. His father had been the first to break away from medicine or pharmacy and enter the bohemian world of the professional artist.

Young Parrish had all the advantages that his financially comfortable family could offer, including taking summer painting trips with his father and visiting the major museums of Europe during his teens. He and Stephen remained close all their lives and were warmly devoted to one another.

Parrish attended Haverford College where he was graduated in 1892 as a Phi Kappa Sigma. He entered Pennsylvania Academy of the Fine Arts in 1892 and stayed there through 1894, auditing some of Howard Pyle's classes at Drexel Institute of Arts and Sciences whenever he could. It was at Drexel that he met an instructor named Lydia Austin (1872–1953), whom he courted and married in 1895. It was in 1895, too, that he received his first cover commission from *Harper's Bazaar*. This important assignment gave him the financial means to marry Lydia when he was twenty-five years old. The marriage produced four children: John Dillwyn (1904), Maxfield Jr. (1906), Stephen (1909), and Jean (1911).

Parrish began illustrating children's books in 1897 when he was approached by publishers Way and Williams of Chicago to illustrate L. Frank Baum's first work, *Mother Goose in Prose*. (This work remains one of the most valuable of all the Parrish illustrated books with a first edition now fetching between $1,500 and $2,000.) The success of the book prompted another publisher, R. H. Russell of New York, to solicit Parrish's work for a new edition of Washington Irving's *Knickerbocker's History of New York* in 1898 (published in 1900).

The financial gains from these books brought Parrish the income to allow him to move away from Philadelphia and to New Hampshire to join his father and other major artists, including Augustus Saint-Gaudens, Winston Churchill (the American writer), Percy McKay, Frederic Remington, and others in a famous artists' colony located between Cornish and

Plainfield, New Hampshire. In 1899 publisher John Lane of London and New York asked Parrish to illustrate Kenneth Grahame's books *The Golden Age* (1899) and *Dream Days* (1902). The international success of these children's classics brought Parrish still another major publisher, Charles Scribner's Sons in New York, who published three of this century's best-loved children's books. The Scribner titles—Eugene Field's *Poems of Childhood* (1904), Kate Douglas Wiggin's and Nora A. Smith's *The Arabian Nights: Their Best-Known Tales* (1909), and Louise Saunders's *The Knave of Hearts* (1925)—remain to this day the best known of Parrish's illustrated books.

Parrish's success in book illustration was perhaps also due to his love of books. He was a voracious reader, carefully nurturing his own children's reading habits. His magnificent home, "The Oaks," located on a hill overlooking a twenty-mile view of the Connecticut River valley, contained a wonderfully paneled upstairs library lined with books from floor to ceiling, and cozy window seats inviting the reader to curl up comfortably with a book. Below in the formal twenty-by-forty-feet music and living room, the east wall facing his baronial fireplace was also filled with his treasured books. In his studio across from the main house, ample shelving had been built to provide the artist with reference and inspirational material. Music, too, was very much a part of his daily life. Musical soirees were held often in the main house, which this versatile man had designed and built himself.

Parrish's popularity led other major authors to want his illustrations in their books. Edith Wharton's *Italian Villas and Their Gardens* (1904) and Nathaniel Hawthorne's *A Wonder-Book and Tanglewood Tales* (1910) are still sought out today because of the Parrish illustrations. Many of his book illustrations were also used as covers for magazines such as *Collier's*, *Ladies' Home Journal*, *Hearst's*, and *Century*. Advertisers innundated him with requests for art. It is estimated that Parrish delivered over one billion advertising messages for Edison Mazda (the precursor of General Electric), Jello, Fiske Tire, Djer Kiss Perfume, Ferry Seed, and countless others.

Parrish was brought into millions of American homes via his book illustrations, his advertisements, his calendars and greeting cards, and his famous art prints. The House of Art in New York and Dodge Publishing brought out art prints including the famous *Daybreak*, *Garden of Allah*, *The Dinkey-Bird*, and countless others. Brown and Bigelow in St. Paul, Minnesota, specialized in producing Parrish landscapes for their calendars and greeting cards. In 1925 it was estimated that one out of every five American homes had a Parrish print on its wall. He remains the most-reproduced artist in the history of American art.

Parrish's paintings are owned by such great institutions as The Metropolitan Museum of Art, the M. H. De Young Memorial Museum, The Charles Hosmer Morse Museum of American Art, and The Detroit Institute of Arts, attesting to the fact that Parrish made the transition from illustration to fine art quite effortlessly.

One thing is certain: Parrish's works continue to beguile and delight readers and viewers of all ages. He is the perpetual Pied Piper, luring and cajoling us into his special land of make-believe and enchanted fantasy.

OLD KING COLE

TRADITIONAL MOTHER GOOSE RHYME

Old King Cole

Was a merry old soul,
and a merry old soul was he;
He called for his pipe,
And he called for his bowl,
And he called for his fiddlers three.

Every fiddler, he had a fiddle,
And a very fine fiddle had he;
Twee tweedle dee, tweedle dee, went the fiddlers.
Oh, there's none so rare
As can compare
With King Cole and his fiddlers three.

THE FROG PRINCE

BY THE BROTHERS GRIMM   RETOLD BY ALMA GILBERT

Once upon a time in a castle in a faraway land there lived a beautiful princess named Pearl. One day she was playing with a golden ball that her father the king had given her, when *plop!* the ball fell into a deep, dark pond.

The young princess sat by the pond and began to cry. The ball was expensive and one of her favorite toys. Suddenly a big frog popped out from the murky depths and asked the princess if she'd like her toy back. Princess Pearl was delighted and promised the frog to be his best friend forever if he retrieved her ball. In a twinkle, the great frog was back, but before he could waddle out of the pond, the princess had snatched her precious ball and run back to the castle.

That evening, while they were having dinner, who should appear at the banquet table but the ugly frog. When the princess told the king that she had promised to be the frog's friend forever, he insisted his daughter honor her promise and allow the frog to sit by her and have his meal alongside the family. At the end of the evening when it came time to retire, Princess Pearl ran up the stairs to her room, seeking to avoid her ugly companion. But no! It was not to be. Soon the frog could be heard knocking at her door, begging to be let in because he was tired. The frog plopped himself on Princess Pearl's bed and there he stayed.

The frog repeated this behavior night after night for seven long evenings. On the seventh night he asked the princess for a kiss. In anger Princess Pearl threw him out of the room, but he cried so plaintively that she took pity on him and opened her door. Touched by the sincerity of the frog's tears, the young princess bent down and kissed his head.

No sooner had she done this, when—lo and behold! before her eyes, the frog disappeared and a handsome young prince knelt before her.

"Oh, dear Princess!" he said. "You have saved me from a wicked witch's spell. I would not kiss her, so she turned me into an ugly frog until someone should take pity on me and kiss me despite my ugliness."

Princess Pearl was quite taken by this charming prince. Her father gave them permission to marry and they lived happily ever after, rewarding all acts of kindness performed by their subjects for those in need—and that, dear children, is what happiness is all about.

THE GOLDEN FLEECE

BY NATHANIEL HAWTHORNE   RETOLD BY ALMA GILBERT

Jason, the son of dethroned King Aeson, was challenged by his uncle, the wicked King Pelias, to prove his worthiness to his father's throne. Pelias required that Jason should perform an act of bravery, specifically that he find and bring back the Golden Fleece. This was the coat of a ram that had died saving a boy's life. The gods had rewarded the ram by turning its coat into brilliant golden fleece, and this coat was guarded by two raging, fire-breathing bulls, a fire-breathing dragon, and an army of warriors from the dragon's teeth.

Jason sought the advice of an oracle found deep in a forest. The oracle was known as the Talking Oak because the gods had chosen to give it that material form. The Talking Oak suggested Jason have a ship built for him by Argus the shipbuilder. The oracle also counseled that the ship be equipped with fifty of the bravest men of Greece, including Hercules, Castor, and Pollux. The prow of the ship, named the Argo, should be fashioned from a limb of the Talking Oak to guide and encourage the Argonauts in their journey to find the Golden Fleece.

The Argonauts reached the island of Colchis ruled by cruel King Aeëtes. Aeëtes warned Jason that before reaching the Golden Fleece, he had to yoke two fire-breathing bulls to help him sow dragon's teeth, from which an army of warriors would spring up.

Fortunately for Jason, the king's daughter, Medea, was an enchantress who took a liking to Jason and his Argonauts and decided to help them. She provided him with a balm to keep him from being scorched by the fire-breathing bulls and dragon. Armed with this, Jason controlled the bulls and proceeded to his next task: overcoming the warriors of the dragon's teeth.

Medea counseled Jason to cast a stone among the warriors. Confused, they would fight and destroy one another.

Jason was ready to face his final task before reaching the Golden Fleece: to slay the dragon that guarded the pelt. Again Medea came to his rescue and gave him a vial containing a powerful sleeping potion. Instead of killing the fire-breathing monster, Jason threw the vial at him and the dragon fell to the ground in a deep sleep.

Jason stepped over the sleeping dragon and approached the radiant Golden Fleece. He freed it from its fastenings and hurried back to his ship and his Argonauts. Having escaped

from the pursuing Aeëtes, Jason returned home triumphantly with the Golden Fleece. By his courage and wisdom he had rightfully earned his father's throne. Pelias was dethroned and Jason ruled, helped by his friends the Argonauts and his oracle, the Talking Oak.

From *Tanglewood Tales for Girls and Boys; being a second Wonder-Book*. (Ticknor, 1853).

THE PIED PIPER OF HAMELIN

BY ROBERT BROWNING

I

Hamelin Town's in Brunswick
By famous Hanover city;
    The river Weser, deep and wide,
    Washes its wall on the southern side;
    A pleasanter spot you never spied;
But, when begins my ditty,
    Almost five hundred years ago,
    To see the townsfolk suffer so
        From vermin, was a pity.

II

Rats!
They fought the dogs and killed the cats,
    And bit the babies in the cradles,
And ate the cheeses out of the vats,
    And licked the soup from the cooks' own ladles,
Split open the kegs of salted sprats,
Made nests inside men's Sunday hats,
And even spoiled the women's chats
        By drowning their speaking
        With shrieking and squeaking
In fifty different sharps and flats.

III

At last the people in a body
    To the Town Hall came flocking:
" 'Tis clear," cried they, "our Mayor's a noddy;
    And as for our Corporation—shocking
To think we buy gowns lined with ermine
For dolts that can't or won't determine

What's best to rid us of our vermin!
You hope, because you're old and obese,
To find in the furry civic robe ease?
Rouse up, sirs! Give your brains a racking
To find the remedy we're lacking,
Or, sure as fate, we'll send you packing!"
At this the Mayor and Corporation
Quaked with a mighty consternation.

IV

An hour they sat in council;
        At length the Mayor broke silence:
"For a guilder I'd my ermine gown sell.
    I wish I were a mile hence!
It's easy to bid one rack one's brain—
I'm sure my poor head aches again,
I've scratched it so, and all in vain.
Oh for a trap, a trap, a trap!"
Just as he said this, what should hap
At the chamber-door but a gentle tap?
"Bless us," cried the Mayor, "what's that?"
(With the Corporation as he sat,
Looking little though wondrous fat;
Nor brighter was his eye, not moister
Than a too-long-opened oyster,
Save when at noon his paunch grew mutinous
For a plate of turtle green and glutinous.)
"Only a scraping of shoes on the mat?
Anything like the sound of a rat
Makes my heart go pit-a-pat!"

V
"Come in!"—the Mayor cried, looking bigger:
    And in did come the strangest figure!
His queer long coat from heel to head
Was half of yellow and half of red,
And he himself was tall and thin,
With sharp blue eyes, each like a pin,
And light loose hair, yet swarthy skin,
No tuft on cheek nor beard on chin,
But lips where smiles went out and in;
There was no guessing his kith and kin:
And nobody could enough admire
The tall man and his quaint attire.
Quoth one: "It's as my great-grandsire,
Starting up at the Trump of Doom's tone,
Had walked this way from his painted tombstone!"

VI
He advanced to the council-table:
    "Please your honors," said he, "I am able,
By means of a secret charm, to draw
All creatures living beneath the sun,
That creep or swim or fly or run,
After me so as you never saw!
And I chiefly use my charm
On creatures that do people harm,
The mole and toad and newt and viper;
And people call me the Pied Piper."
(And here they noticed round his neck
A scarf of red and yellow stripe,
To match with his coat of the self-same cheque
And at the scarf's end hung a pipe;
And his fingers, they noticed, were ever straying
As if impatient to be playing
Upon this pipe, as low it dangled
Over his vesture so old-fangled.)
"Yet," said he, "poor piper as I am,
In Tartary I freed the Cham,
Last June, from his huge swarms of gnats;

I eased in Asia the Nizam
Of a monstrous brood of vampire-bats:
And as for what your brain bewilders,
If I can rid your town of rats
Will you give me a thousand guilders?"
"One? fifty thousand!"—was the exclamation
Of the astonished Mayor and Corporation.

VII
Into the street the Piper stept,
    Smiling first a little smile
As if he knew what magic slept
    In his quiet pipe the while;
Then, like a musical adept,
To blow the pipe his lips he wrinkled,
And green and blue his sharp eyes twinkled,
Like a candle-flame where salt is sprinkled;
And ere three shrill notes the pipe uttered,
You heard as if an army muttered;
And the muttering grew to a grumbling;
And the grumbling grew to a mighty rumbling;
And out of the houses the rats came tumbling.
Great rats, small rats, lean rats, brawny rats,
Brown rats, black rats, gray rats, tawny rats.
Grave old plodders, gay young friskers,
    Fathers, mothers, uncles, cousins,
Cocking tails and pricking whiskers,
    Families by tens and dozens,
Brothers, sisters, husbands, wives—
Followed the Piper for their lives.
From street to street he piped advancing,
And step for step they followed dancing,
Until they came to the river Weser,
Wherin all plunged and perished!
—Save one who, stout as Julius Caesar,
Swam across and lived to carry
(As he, the manuscript he cherished)
To Rat-land home his commentary:

Which was, "At the first shrill notes of the pipe,
I heard a sound as of scraping tripe,
And putting apples, wondrous ripe,
Into a cider-press's gripe:
And a moving away of pickle-tub-boards,
And a leaving ajar of conserve-cupboards,
And a drawing the corks of train-oil-flasks,
And a breaking the hoops of butter-casks:
And it seemed as if a voice
(Sweeter far than by harp or by psaltery
Is breathed) called out, 'Oh rats, rejoice!
The world is grown to one vast drysaltery!
So munch on, crunch on, take your nuncheon,
Breakfast, supper, dinner, luncheon!'
And just as a bulky sugar-puncheon
All ready staved, like a great sun shone
Glorious scarce an inch before me,
Just as methought it said, 'Come, bore me!'
—I found the Weser rolling o'er me."

VIII You should have heard the Hamelin people
Ringing the bells till they rocked the
steeple.
"Go," cried the Mayor, "and get long poles,
Poke out the nests and block up the holes!
Consult with carpenters and builders,
And leave in our town not even a trace
Of the rats!"—when suddenly, up the face
Of the Piper perked in the market-place,
With a, "First, if you please, my thousand guilders!"

IX A thousand guilders! The Mayor looked blue;
So did the Corporation too.
For council dinners made rare havoc
With Claret, Moselle, Vin-de-Grave, Hock;
And half the money would replenish
Their cellar's biggest butt with Rhenish.
To pay this sum to a wandering fellow

THE PIED PIPER

With a gypsy coat of red and yellow!
"Beside," quoth the Mayor with a knowing wink,
"Our business was done at the river's brink;
We saw with our eyes the vermin sink,
And what's dead can't come to life, I think.
So, friend,we're not the folks to shrink
From the duty of giving you something for drink,
And a matter of money to put in your poke;
But as for the guilders, what we spoke
Of them, as you very well know, was in joke.
Besides our losses have made us thrifty.
A thousand guilders! Come, take fifty!"

X The Piper's face fell, and he cried,
"No trifling! I can't wait, beside!
I've promised to visit by dinner time
Bagdat, and accept the prime
Of the Head-Cook's pottage, all he's rich in,
For having left, in the Caliph's kitchen,

Of a nest of scorpions no survivor:
With him I proved no bargain-driver,
With you, don't think I'll bate a stiver!
And folks who put me in a passion
May find me pipe after another fashion."

XI "How?" cried the Mayor, "d'ye think I brook
Being worse treated than a Cook?
Insulted by a lazy ribald
With idle pipe and vesture piebald?
You threaten us, fellow? Do your worst,
Blow your pipe there till you burst!"

XII Once more he stept into the street,
And to his lips again
Laid his long pipe of smooth straight cane;
And ere he blew three notes (such sweet
Soft notes as yet musician's cunning
Never gave the enraptured air)
There was a rustling that seemed like a bustling
Of merry crowds justling at pitching and hustling;
Small feet were pattering, wooden shoes clattering,
Little hands clapping and little tongues chattering,
And, like fowls in a farm-yard when barley scattering,
Out came the children running.
All the little boys and girls,
With rosy cheeks and flaxen curls,
And sparkling eyes and teeth like pearls,
Tripping and skipping, ran merrily after
The wonderful music with shouting and laughter.

XIII The Mayor was dumb, and the Council stood
As if they were changed into blocks of wood.
Unable to move a step, or cry
To the children merrily skipping by,
—Could only follow with the eye
That joyous crowd at the Piper's back.

But how the Mayor was on the rack,
And the wretched Council's bosoms beat,
As the Piper turned from the High Street
To where the Weser rolled its waters
Right in the way of their sons and daughters.
However, he turned from South to West,
And to Koppelberg Hill his steps addressed,
And after him the children pressed;
Great was the joy in every breast.
"He never can cross that mighty top!
He's forced to let the piping drop,
And we shall see our children stop!"
When, lo, as they reached the mountain-side,
A wondrous portal opened wide,
As if a cavern was suddenly hollowed;
And the Piper advanced and the children followed,
And when all were in to the very last,
The door in the mountain-side shut fast.
Did I say, all? No! One was lame,
And could not dance the whole of the way;
And in after years, if you would blame
His sadness, he was used to say,—
"It's dull in our town since my playmates left:
I can't forget that I'm bereft
Of all the pleasant sights they see,
Which the Piper also promised me.
For he led us, he said, to a joyous land,
Joining the town and just at hand,
Where waters gushed and fruit-trees grew
And flowers put forth a fairer hue,
And everything was strange and new;
The sparrows were brighter than peacocks here
And their dogs outran our fallow deer,
And honey-bees had lost their stings,
And horses were born with eagles' wings:
And just as I became assured
My lame foot would be speedily cured,
The music stopped and I stood still,
And found myself outside the hill,
Left alone against my will,
To go now limping as before,
And never hear of that country more."

XIV Alas, alas for Hamelin!
          There came into many a burgher's pate
       A text which says that heaven's gate
          Opes to the rich at as easy rate
As the needle's eye takes a camel in!
The Mayor sent East, West, North and South
To offer the Piper, by word of mouth,
       Wherever it was men's lot to find him,
Silver and gold to his heart's content,
If he'd only return the way he went,
       And bring the children behind him.
But when they saw 'twas a lost endeavor,
And Piper and dancers were gone forever,
They made a decree that lawyers never
       Should think their records dated duly
If, after the day of the month and year,
These words did not as well appear.
"And so long after what happened here
       On the Twenty-second of July,
Thirteen hundred and seventy-six":
And the better in memory to fix
The place of the children's last retreat,
They called it, the Pied Piper's Street—
Where any one playing on pipe or tabor
Was sure for the future to lose his labor.
Nor suffered they hostelry or tavern
       To shock with mirth a street so solemn
But opposite the place of the cavern
       They wrote the story on a column.

HUMPTY DUMPTY

TRADITIONAL MOTHER GOOSE RHYME

Humpty Dumpty sat on a wall;
Humpty Dumpty had a great fall.
    All the king's horses
    And all the king's men
Couldn't put Humpty Dumpty together again.

CINDERELLA

BY CHARLES PERRAULT   RETOLD BY ALMA GILBERT

Once upon a time in a faraway land, there lived a prosperous merchant who had a lovely daughter. After his wife died, the merchant married a woman who had two daughters of her own. The stepmother and two stepsisters were very unkind and cruel to the merchant's young daughter, making her do all the menial tasks around the house, including cleaning the ashes and cinders from the fireplace. The stepmother nicknamed the poor sister Cinderella.

One day an announcement came from the palace. The king's son was looking for a bride and a big ball was to be held in his honor to present all the marriageable young ladies of the land to him. The wicked stepmother and the cruel stepsisters began feverishly preparing for the ball, ignoring poor Cinderella.

Cinderella wanted to go, too, and on the night of the ball, after her wicked stepsisters had left to meet the prince, she sobbed silently by the fireplace. Suddenly, in a flash, her beautiful fairy godmother appeared, and touching her with a magic wand turned Cinderella's clothing into a ball gown shimmering with threads of gold. With another wave of her wand, Cinderella's godmother turned a pumpkin and seven little scurrying mice into a coach and footmen. Only one thing was asked of Cinderella: that she return to the house before midnight, when the spell would be broken and her gown and coach and footmen would disappear.

Cinderella had a lovely time at the ball and quite captured the prince's heart. Time sped by quickly and before she knew it the large clock in the belfry began chiming midnight. Quickly Cinderella sped down the palace stairs, leaving in her haste one of the lovely crystal slippers given her by the fairy godmother. Cinderella arrived home at the final stroke of midnight. Just as the fairy godmother had predicted, her beautiful dress and the coach and footmen all disappeared.

The prince, saddened by the sudden departure of the lovely young woman who had captured his heart, issued a proclamation that he would wed the lovely lady whose dainty foot fit the crystal slipper.

In vain the prince's footmen searched high and low for a young lady whose foot fit the tiny slipper. They finally approached Cinderella's house. The wicked stepsisters tried the slipper on but to no avail. Emboldened by the sight of the prince who had captured her heart, Cinderella asked to try on the slipper, also.

To everyone's astonishment, it fit her perfectly. The prince recognized in the shy young woman the lovely partner who had captured his heart. Falling before her, he proposed marriage and, of course, Cinderella accepted. We are told that they lived happily together for years and years and were revered and loved by all of their subjects.

THE DINKEY-BIRD

BY EUGENE FIELD

In an ocean, 'way out yonder
    (As all sapient people know),
Is the land of Wonder-Wander,
    Whither children love to go;
It's their playing, romping, swinging,
    That give great joy to me
While the Dinkey-Bird goes singing
    In the amfalula tree!

There the gum-drops grow like cherries,
    And taffy's thick as peas—
Caramels you pick like berries
    When, and where, and how you please;
Big red sugar-plums are clinging
    To the cliffs beside that sea
Where the Dinkey-Bird is singing
    In the amfalula tree.

So when children shout and scamper
    And make merry all the day,
When there's naught to put a damper
    To the ardor of their play;
When I hear their laughter ringing,
    Then I'm sure as sure can be
That the Dinkey-Bird is singing
    In the amfalula tree.

For the Dinkey-Bird's bravuras
    And staccatos are so sweet—
His roulades, appoggiaturas,
    And robustos so complete,
That the youth of every nation—
    Be they near or far away—
Have especial delectation
    In that gladsome roundelay.

Their eyes grow bright and brighter
    Their lungs begin to crow,
Their hearts get light and lighter,
    And their cheeks are all aglow;
For an echo cometh bringing
    The news to all and me,
That the Dinkey-Bird is singing
    In the amfalula tree.

I'm sure you like to go there
    To see your feathered friend—
And so many goodies grow there
    You would like to comprehend!
Speed, little dreams, your winging
    To that land across the sea
Where the Dinkey-Bird is singing
    In the amfalula tree!

ALADDIN AND
THE AFRICAN MAGICIAN

RETOLD BY ALMA GILBERT

Once upon a time in an ancient kingdom of China lived the widow of a poor tailor with her son, Aladdin. The widow worried excessively that her only child might not amount to much, since work did not appeal to him and he was uninterested in following his father's trade.

One day while Aladdin was outside playing with other boys his age, an imposing stranger approached him and inquired if he could possibly be the son of Mustapha the tailor. The stranger identified himself as Mustapha's only brother, who had spent the last few years in Africa and had missed his brother's funeral.

In reality, the stranger was not Aladdin's uncle but a very powerful magician who had devious plans for the young man. He suggested to Aladdin and his mother that Aladdin should apprentice under him to become a merchant. Both agreed and Aladdin and the magician were soon on their way. They traveled for many days until they came to the edge of a mountain.

Here the magician bade his young apprentice to gather wood and build a fire. When Aladdin had done so, the magician drew from his robes a box of perfumed oils. Casting them upon the fire, he murmured strange words and intoned incantations. As he spoke, the sky darkened and the earth opened at his feet showing a flat stone, adorned only by a brass ring.

The magician told Aladdin that under that stone was a great treasure, greater than any owned by an earthly king. He warned Aladdin that to obtain it, he must follow instructions to the letter. Aladdin did as he was told. He lifted the slab by pulling the ring with all his might. The gaping hole uncovered a staircase leading down into the bowels of the earth. The African magician instructed Aladdin to descend until he found a garden where jewels grew on trees like fruit. He warned Aladdin not to touch anything until he came to a place where a solitary lamp hung. Aladdin was to bring the lamp back. The magician gave the young man his ring and instructed him to wear it to ward off evil spirits lurking below.

The precious jeweled garden was as the magician had described. The jewels were of a size and brilliance beyond all of Aladdin's dreams. At last he came to end of a cavern. In a niche was the lamp he had been instructed to find. Aladdin filled his pockets with every precious jewel that he could carry and headed up back to the opening.

The magician told Aladdin to pass up the lamp first, and then he would help him out of the cave. But Aladdin wanted to be helped out before turning over the lamp. In a fit of anger the magician conjured up a spell which caused the slab to fall back into place trapping Aladdin below.

The magician had tried to use the young man to fetch the magic lamp since he himself was prevented by the curse of another enchanter from entering the hidden-treasure cave. Now, angry and frustrated, the magician left in disappointment, vowing to return the following year with a new apprentice to brave the spells of the cave. In his haste to depart, however, he had forgotten about the ring he had given Aladdin.

Meanwhile, poor Aladdin despaired of ever seeing the light of day again. In anguish he wrung his hands and accidentally rubbed the ring that his "uncle" had given him. To his utter amazement and fright, a monstrous genie appeared before him, proclaiming himself Aladdin's servant, ready to do his bidding.

Of course Aladdin's bidding was to get out of the cave. With a clap of thunder, the genie obeyed and the startled youngster found himself standing outside, laden with the jeweled fruit and the magic lamp. Of all the treasures possible none could compare with those to be found within the lamp, which housed a genie even more powerful than the one in the magic ring.

Aladdin and his mother lived in wealth and happiness the rest of their days, proud possessors of the lamp, which eventually also brought him the sultan's daughter for his bride. But that, dear children, is another story.

From *The Arabian Nights: Their Best-Known Tales*, edited by Kate Douglas Wiggin and Nora A. Smith (Charles Scribner's Sons, 1909).

PETER, PETER, PUMPKIN-EATER

TRADITIONAL MOTHER GOOSE RHYME

Peter, Peter, pumpkin-eater,
    Had a wife and couldn't keep her;
He put her in a pumpkin shell,
And there he kept her very well.

Peter, Peter, pumpkin-eater,
Had another and didn't love her;
Peter learned to read and spell,
And then he loved her very well.

THE SUGAR-PLUM TREE

BY EUGENE FIELD

Have you ever heard of the Sugar-Plum Tree?
  'Tis a marvel of great renown!
It blooms on the shore of the Lollipop sea
  In the garden of Shut-Eye Town;
The fruit that it bears is so wondrously sweet
  (As those who have tasted it say)
That good little children have only to eat
  Of that fruit to be happy next day.

When you've got to the tree,
    you would have a hard time
  To capture the fruit which I sing;
The tree is so tall that no person could climb
  To the boughs where the sugar-plums swing!
But up in that tree sits a chocolate cat,
  And a gingerbread dog prowls below—
And this is the way you contrive to get at
  Those sugar-plums tempting you so:

You say but the word to that gingerbread dog
  And he barks with such terrible zest
That the chocolate cat is at once all agog,
  As her swelling proportions attest.
And the chocolate cat goes cavorting around
  From this leafy limb unto that,
And the sugar-plums tumble, of course, to the ground—
  Hurrah for that chocolate cat!

There are marshmallows, gumdrops, and
    peppermint canes,
  With stripings of scarlet or gold,
And you carry away of the treasure that rains
  As much as your apron can hold!
So come, little child, cuddle closer to me
  In your dainty white nightcap and gown,
And I'll rock you away to that Sugar-Plum Tree
  In the garden of Shut-Eye Town.

THE DRAGON'S TEETH

BY NATHANIEL HAWTHORNE   RETOLD BY ALMA GILBERT

P rince Cadmus together with his brothers, Phoenix and Cilix, had set out along with their mother, Queen Telephassa, to find their beloved sister, Europa, who had been kidnapped from their midst by the god Zeus in the guise of a bull. For years, they had traveled the kingdom of Phoenicia vainly searching for their beautiful sister.

One by one the older brothers wearied of the journey and stayed behind, becoming kings of the territories they occupied. Cadmus alone continued in the journey until his dear mother, Queen Telephassa, overcome by grief and weariness, died without finding her beloved daughter, Europa.

Cadmus consulted an oracle in Delphi, who instructed him to follow a sacred cow to a spot where he would meet his destiny. Cadmus spotted a brindled cow grazing in a verdant pasture and proceeded to follow its wanderings until they came upon a pleasant meadow surrounded by towering mountains. On this site Cadmus later built the city of Thebes. Attacked by a ferocious dragon, Cadmus fought the beast and slew it with his mighty sword.

The goddess Athena advised Cadmus to sow some of the dragon's teeth; from the teeth sprang up armed men. (Athena later gave the remaining teeth to the Greek hero Jason when he was seeking the Golden Fleece.) Cadmus threw stones into the midst of the warriors who, thinking they were being attacked from within, began to fight among themselves.

Cadmus became the leader of the surviving warriors, who helped him build his city. As a reward for his fidelity to his mother's memory and his fruitless quest for his sister Europa, the gods sent Cadmus a beautiful wife named Harmonia.

Just as his bride's name implied, Cadmus and Harmonia lived in peace and tranquillity ever after, guarded by the warrior sons of the dragon's teeth.

From *Tanglewood Tales for Girls and Boys; being a second Wonder-Book* (Ticknor, 1853).

WYNKEN, BLYNKEN, AND NOD

BY EUGENE FIELD

Wynken, Blynken, and Nod one night
    Sailed off in a wooden shoe—
Sailed on a river of crystal light,
Into a sea of dew.
"Where are you going, and what do you wish?"
    The old moon asked the three.
"We have come to fish for the herring fish
    That live in this beautiful sea;
    Nets of silver and gold have we!"
        Said Wynken,
        Blynken,
        And Nod.

The old moon laughed and sang a song,
    As they rocked in the wooden shoe,
And the wind that sped them all night long
    Ruffled the waves of dew.
The little stars were the herring fish
    That lived in that beautiful sea—
"Now cast your nets wherever you wish—
    Never afeard are we";
    So cried the stars to the fishermen three:
        Wynken,
        Blynken,
        And Nod.

All night long their nets they threw
    To the stars in the twinkling foam—
Then down from the skies came the wooden shoe,
    Bringing the fishermen home;
'Twas all so pretty a sail it seemed
    As if it could not be,
And some folks thought 'twas a dream they'd dreamed
    Of sailing that beautiful sea—
    But I shall name you the fishermen three:
        Wynken,
        Blynken,
        And Nod.

Wynken and Blynken are two little eyes,
    And Nod is a little head,
And the wooden shoe that sailed the skies
    Is a wee one's trundle-bed.

So shut your eyes while mother sings
    Of wonderful sights that be,
And you shall see the beautiful things
    As you rock in the misty sea,
    Where the old shoe rocked the fishermen three:
        Wynken,
        Blynken,
        And Nod.

SNOW WHITE AND THE SEVEN DWARFS

BY THE BROTHERS GRIMM   RETOLD BY ALMA GILBERT

O nce upon a time in a faraway land there lived a king whose beautiful daughter was named Snow White because she had been born one winter morning when the land was blanketed by a brilliant snowfall. Her skin was the color of newly fallen snow, her lips red as rubies, and her hair as gold as the treasures of the richest pharaoh.

Snow White's beauty made her wicked stepmother very jealous, so she ordered her head huntsman to take the innocent child to the forest, slay her, pretend she had been killed by a beast, and bring back her heart.

The huntsman could not do this wicked deed. Instead he told the young princess to flee for her life and brought the wicked queen the heart of a stag.

Meanwhile, Snow White wandered about through the forest, fearful and saddened until she came upon a cottage owned by seven industrious dwarfs who worked in the forest. She busied herself arranging and cleaning the little house. When the dwarfs came home they were so impressed by the neatness of the cottage and the wonderful aromas coming from the oven that they invited Snow White to stay with them permanently.

All would have been well, except that Snow White's stepmother had a magic mirror which she consulted daily to see if she were the most beautiful person in the kingdom. The mirror told her truthfully "No" since Snow White was still alive.

The enraged queen disguised herself as an old woman, packed a basket of apples, making sure to poison them first, and set off to find Snow White. Following the magic mirror's directions to the dwarfs' cottage, the wicked queen knocked on the door and asked for a glass of water. When kind Snow White invited her to come in and rest, she proffered the poisoned apple as a thank-you gift for Snow White's kindness.

The dear princess took one bite and fell silent and still to the floor. The seven dwarfs were heartbroken upon finding their beautiful friend poisoned by the wicked queen. They chased the queen down a ravine, where not even her magic could help her. In her haste to flee from the pursuing dwarfs, she fell backward and broke her neck.

The dwarfs built their dear friend a magnificent glass casket. They were standing by the bier mourning their loss when a handsome prince rode by. Taken by the beauty of the still figure, he asked permission to kiss her lips in homage to her beauty. Oh, wonder of wonders! As this kiss touched her lips, Snow White issued a little gasp, and the piece of poisoned apple lodged in her throat came flying out. The seven dwarfs rejoiced mightily to see that their friend was still alive. As for Snow White and the prince, they live happily ever after, visiting the dwarfs often, and bringing them gifts of her delicious baking, including plenty of apple pies!

THE THREE GOLDEN APPLES

BY NATHANIEL HAWTHORNE   RETOLD BY ALMA GILBERT

In days of old, Hercules, a mighty and noble youth, had been sent by his people in search of the Hesperides and the three mythical Golden Apples, guarded by a many-headed dragon. During his travels, he encountered a giant as tall as a mountain named Atlas, after the mountain where he had been born. The giant was so huge that his head reached the sky and clouds rested around his middle like a girdle. The giant held up his great hands and appeared to be supporting the sky with them, the main weight of the firmament resting on his head and shoulders.

Hercules was a powerfully strong man himself, but nothing to compete with giant Atlas's strength. At least holding up the sky didn't appear to be as dangerous a job as battling a dragon for the Golden Apples. Hercules asked Atlas to trade places with him and battle the dragon while Hercules held up his end of the bargain and shouldered the skies.

Atlas, who had wearied of supporting the firmament, agreed readily. He found the many-headed dragon, and given his mighty size was able to vanquish it without any strain. He collected the Golden Apples and returned to the spot in the mountains where Hercules awaited Atlas's return with the weight of the world sitting on his shoulders. Hercules then tricked Atlas into going back to his position of holding up the sky. He asked Atlas to relieve him momentarily and promised to be right back. Poor Atlas! Before he could complain, Hercules traded places with him, scooped up the Golden Apples, and left, the weight of the sky again resting on Atlas's shoulders.

To this day, there is a mountain in Greece named Atlas whose highest spot appears to disappear into the clouds. When thunder rumbles about its summit, one may imagine it is the voice of poor Atlas bellowing after Hercules to come back and help him hold up the sky.

From *A Wonder-Book for Girls and Boys* (Ticknor, 1852).

THE TALKING BIRD, THE SINGING TREE, AND THE GOLDEN WATER

RETOLD BY ALMA GILBERT

Once upon a time in the kingdom of Persia there lived a sultan named Kosrouschah. One evening while strolling through the streets of his city, he spied three sisters talking. All three were unusually beautiful, but the youngest was of such great beauty that the sultan could not help staring at her. He asked his grand vizier to summon the three sisters to the palace the next day. There it was announced to them that the two older ones would be given in marriage to servants of the ruler, but that the younger one would marry the sultan himself.

This caused tremendous envy and resentment in the older sisters and they vowed to take vengeance. They attended the queen during the birth of her three children: two sons and a daughter. They informed the sultan that his wife had given birth, first, to a dog, then to a cat, and finally to a piece of wood. In reality the three babes were healthy, beautiful, bright children whom the wicked sisters had abandoned in a canal. The angry sultan ordered the queen exiled and imprisoned. Fortunately, the children the queen had borne had been adopted and raised by the chief gardener to the sultan. He spared no effort to educate them in the manner of princes since their abilities far exceeded those of other children of the day. The boys were named Bahman and Perviz. The beautiful little girl was named Periezade. The children grew in beauty, kindness, and courtliness and served their adoptive parent well until the time of his death.

One day an older, wizened woman visited Periezade and told her of three great wonders missing from her beautiful abode which would complete the gardens her dear-departed adoptive father had built. They were the Talking Bird, the Singing Tree, and the Golden Water. Wishing to honor their dead father's memory, Bahman and Perviz started out in search of these treasures but fell victim to the curse which protected them. The young men, like many others who had tried to find the treasures, were turned to stone when they came close to achieving their goal.

Periezade became aware of the fate which had befallen her brothers. She decided that life would have no meaning for her if she did not try to find and rescue those so dear to her. She would also try to find the treasure that had eluded them. Stuffing her ears with cotton, she followed her brothers' path. Unable to hear the malediction and curses of the evil spirits that had led to the princes' downfall, she was able to climb to the mountaintop where the Talking Bird was imprisoned in a golden cage. She freed the bird, who then became her slave and endeavored to help her.

The Talking Bird showed her the site of the Golden Water, which she stored in a flask she carried for just such a purpose. Following the bird's advice, she found the site of the Singing Tree from which she cut a branch. Coming down from the mountain, Periezade sprinkled the water on all of the stones along her way. They were immediately converted into the men who had been enchanted. To her joy, both of her brothers were among those freed from the spell. In gratitude, all of the men she had saved declared themselves her slaves and followers.

The happy party returned to their home. The Singing Tree, the Talking Bird, and the Golden Water brought charm and beauty to their already spectacular gardens. News of them spread through the land, and soon even the sultan heard of the gardens and wished to visit them.

The sultan was so taken by the grace and beauty of the property, and by that of its owners, that he invited the princes to join him in his palace for dinner. Bahman and Perviz asked him instead to honor them and their sister by dining at their home.

Periezade consulted the Talking Bird, who advised her to prepare for the sultan a special delicacy made with pearls and cucumbers which only his queen, their mother, had fed him. When the sultan arrived, the royal guest was shown the wonders of the house: the Talking Bird, the fountain that housed the Golden Waters, and the magical Singing Tree. The sultan expressed astonishment at the dish of cucumbers and pearls, and then the Talking Bird recalled to him how easily he had accepted the false stories about the births of his children. The bird then informed him of the true identity of the children of the house; they were his own dear children, the sons and daughters taken from his queen at birth.

The sultan was filled with joy at finding his family, but angry that he had been duped all these years by the wicked sisters. He released his queen, who was rejoined by their children. The sultan fell before her and begged her pardon for the great wrong that had been done to her. The queen, who had never stopped loving him, forgave him. The family returned to the palace in Persia where they lived in happiness, wisdom, and tranquillity to the end of their days.

From *The Arabian Nights: Their Best-Known Tales*, edited by Kate Douglas Wiggin and Nora A. Smith (Charles Scribner's Sons, 1909).

WITH TRUMPET AND DRUM

BY EUGENE FIELD

With big tin trumpet and little red drum,
   Marching like soldiers, the children come!
   It's this way and that way they circle and file—
   My! but that music of theirs is fine!
 This way and that way, and after a while
   They march straight into this heart of mine!
A sturdy old heart, but it has to succumb
To the blare of that trumpet and beat of that drum!

Come on, little people, from cot and from hall—
This heart it hath welcome and room for you all!
   It will sing you its songs and warm you with love,
     As your dear little arms with my arms intertwine;

It will rock you away to the dreamland above—
   Oh, a jolly old heart is this old heart of mine,
And jollier still is it bound to become
When you blow that big trumpet and beat that red drum!

So come; though I see not *his* dear little face
And hear not *his* voice in this jubilant place,
   I know he were happy to bid me enshrine
     His memory deep in my heart with your play—
   Ah me! but a love that is sweeter than mine
     Holdeth my boy in its keeping to-day!
And my heart it is lonely—so, little fold, come,
March in and make merry with trumpet and drum!

THE POMEGRANATE SEEDS

BY NATHANIEL HAWTHORNE   RETOLD BY ALMA GILBERT

P roserpina was the beautiful child of Mother Nature, known to mortals by the name Mother Ceres. One day when Ceres was busy with her chores, she left Proserpina alone to wander to the seashore. There the youngster liked to play and cavort with the sea nymphs who inhabited the shoreline.

Proserpina and the sea nymphs were fashioning necklaces of shells together. After a while the youngster decided to gather flowers to include in sea-shell necklaces for her sea nymphs. She wandered near a magnificent bush with absolutely the most perfect flowers. It beckoned to her with its beauty, practically begging to be picked.

Suddenly, the earth began to tremble and Pluto, king of the Underworld, appeared. Catching Proserpina by the waist, he carried her away to his underground kingdom heedless of her pitiful cries for her mother. At that very moment, aware of danger to her child by her mother's instinct, Ceres was enveloped by an indescribable pang of anxiety. She rushed to the seashore and questioned the sea nymphs as to the whereabouts of her child. Then she retraced the youngster's footsteps to the pasture where Proserpina had been swallowed by the earth.

Disconsolate as only a mother could be, Ceres vowed not to let the earth grow one more flower or crop until her darling daughter was restored to her. Zeus, king of the gods, became alarmed at the dying, parched earth below. He dispatched Mercury to speak to Pluto about releasing Proserpina. The languishing captive had refused to touch any food since her abduction. Pluto had tried all manner of temptations to get the child to eat since if she were to taste the food offered her by Pluto, she would become enslaved by his spell and could never leave.

Pluto tempted her once more with what he knew was Proserpina's favorite fruit: a pomegranate. The child remembered the juicy taste of the ripe fruit in her mother's kitchen and reached out to take a few grains before Zeus's messenger, Mercury, could stop her. Too late! She was now doomed to stay in Pluto's underground kingdom.

King Pluto, who had learned to love the child, was persuaded by Mercury to release her to Mother Ceres so that the earth would once more prosper. Pluto agreed to release her, provided she return to visit him for at least part of the year.

As soon as Proserpina stepped outside of the underground kingdom, the earth bloomed again in all its glory. Mother Ceres agreed to her daughter's promised absences and that was the beginning of the four seasons. During the months that Proserpina was under-

ground, the earth, following Mother Ceres's command, was sad, desolate, and grew nothing until Proserpina's return in April. Then the flowers would again bloom, crops be planted, and youth celebrate their time-honored rites of spring.

From *Tanglewood Tales for Girls and Boys; being a second Wonder-Book* (Ticknor, 1853)

MARY, MARY, QUITE CONTRARY

TRADITIONAL MOTHER GOOSE RHYME

Mary, Mary, quite contrary,
How does your garden grow?
With silver bells and cockle-shells,
And pretty maids, all in a row.

PUSS-IN-BOOTS

BY CHARLES PERRAULT   RETOLD BY ALMA GILBERT

Once upon a time in a faraway land there lived a miller who had three sons. When the miller grew too old to work, he gave his mill to his oldest son, his land to his second son, and his favorite cat, which was all he had left, to his youngest son.

The youngest son was fortunate to be given his father's favorite cat, for this was a magical cat who could talk. The cat, who was also very handsome, asked his new owner to get him an outfit complete with a pair of boots so that he could earn a living for his master. The young son did so, and no sooner had he brought the cat his outfit and boots than the cat went off to catch a rabbit. The cat then hurried to present the rabbit—not to his master—but to the king of the land himself.

The cat told the monarch that the rabbit was a present from his great master the Marquis of Carrabas. Within a month, the cat repeatedly presented the king with gifts, and the cat and his distinctive outfit and boots became well known to the king.

The clever cat found out that the king and his daughter were going to travel in the countryside. Immediately Puss-in-Boots persuaded his master to go swimming in a lake near where the king would pass. While his master swam, Puss took his master's clothes and hid them. At the precise instant the king's carriage came near, Puss sprang out of the bushes and waved it to a stop. "Help! Help! My master, the Marquis of Carrabas, is drowning!" the cat cried. The king recognized Puss-in-Boots, of whom he had become quite fond, and ordered his aides to help the young man.

To his surprise, the miller's son was fished out of the water, given a nice suit of clothing, and presented to the king. He rode in the carriage with the king and his beautiful daughter back to the palace. Meanwhile Puss ran ahead of the king's party to the castle of a ferocious but not very bright giant. The giant possessed vast lands and knew a few magic tricks.

The giant was astonished at the sight of Puss-in-Boots, who convinced him that he, too, was a magician, but certainly not as clever as the giant himself. Puss convinced the giant to turn himself into a cat with clothes, just like himself. This the giant did. Puss then challenged the giant to turn himself into something much smaller because that was more difficult. In a twinkling, the giant turned himself into a little gray mouse. Puss then pounced on the mouse and swallowed it in a flash.

When the king's carriage passed by the now empty castle, Puss was there to greet him and his party. He invited them all to come in and rest as guests of none other than his own master, the Marquis of Carrabas, who, he said, was the owner of all these vast lands. The king was so impressed that he offered to let his beautiful daughter marry the miller's son, now the "Marquis." The couple lived happily in the huge castle along with the clever cat in his handsome outfit and stylish boots.

THE FLY-AWAY HORSE

BY EUGENE FIELD

Oh, a wonderful horse is the Fly-Away Horse—
  Perhaps you have seen him before;
Perhaps, while you slept, his shadow has swept
  Through the moonlight that floats on the floor.
For it's only at night, when the stars twinkle bright,
  That the Fly-Away Horse, with a neigh
And a pull at his rein and a toss of his mane,
  Is up on his heels and away!
      The Moon in the sky,
      As he gallopeth by,
    Cries: "Oh! what a marvellous sight!"
      And the Stars in dismay
      Hide their faces away
    In the lap of old Grandmother Night.

It is yonder, out yonder, the Fly-Away Horse
  Speedeth ever and ever away—
Over meadows and lanes, over mountains and plains,
  Over streamlets that sing at their play;
And over the sea like a ghost sweepeth he,
  While the ships they go sailing below,
And he speedeth so fast that the men at the mast
  Adjudge him some portent of woe.
      "What ho there!" they cry,
      As he flourishes by
    With a whisk of his beautiful tail;
      And the fish in the sea
      Are as scared as can be,
    From the nautilus up to the whale!

And the Fly-Away Horse seeks those far-away lands
  You little folk dream of at night—
Where candy-trees grow, and honey-brooks flow,
  And corn-fields with popcorn are white;
And the beasts in the wood are ever so good
  To children who visit them there—
What glory astride of a lion to ride,
  Or to wrestle around with a bear!
      The monkeys, they say:
      "Come on, let us play,"
    And they frisk in the cocoanut-trees:
      While the parrots, that cling
      To the peanut-vines, sing
    Or converse with comparative ease!

Off! scamper to bed—you shall ride him to-night!
  For, as soon as you've fallen asleep,
With a jubilant neigh he shall bear you away
  Over forest and hillside and deep!
But tell us, my dear, all you see and you hear
  In those beautiful lands over there,
Where the Fly-Away Horse wings his far-away course
  With the wee one consigned to his care.
      Then grandma will cry
      In amazement: "Oh, my!"
    And she'll think it could never be so;
      And only we two
      Shall know it is true—
    You and I, little precious! shall know!

AGIB IN THE ENCHANTED PALACE

RETOLD BY ALMA GILBERT

P rince Agib was the son of a king who ruled his kingdom in justice and happiness. The capital city stood on the shore of a wide sea. The young prince was an accomplished navigator who had undertaken many a voyage.

It was during one of these voyages that his ship was wrecked upon a distant shore and he found himself stranded, exhausted, on a beach. He garnered the strength to begin what was to be a long journey in a strange land. The journey took forty days and forty nights.

At last the destitute prince arrived at a palace gate where he was brought before ten richly clad young men, each blind in one eye. They welcomed him, clothed and fed him. Agib could not contain his curiosity any longer. He asked his hosts about their strange eye maladies. The young men responded that they had all fallen prey to temptation and in so doing had lost their eyes in punishment. They beseeched Agib not to follow their path, but the prince, wishing to repay their hospitality, promised to avenge the loss of their sight.

The youths showed him the entrance to the Palace of Hundred Delights where their losses had occurred. Agib followed their directions and found a mansion that rivalled Paradise. He was met by bowers of flowers, reflecting pools, and forty beautiful maidens.

The maidens informed him that they were there to please him and satisfy all of his needs. After a year the maidens left him for a period of forty days. Before leaving they gave him one hundred keys, each of which would open a closet door in the palace. Agib was given permission to open all but one door, the door of red gold. After marveling at the delights found behind the ninety-nine doors, curiosity got the better of the prince, and he opened the forbidden door!

He was immediately overcome by a sweet perfume which rendered him unconscious. When he awoke, a dazzling black stallion stood towering over him. The prince mounted it without hesitation. The mighty horse reared and with a sound like the roar of thunder, spread a pair of wings and flew, carrying the hapless Agib on his back. After a long journey, the black stallion alighted on a terrace where he flung Agib to the ground. With a violent blow from his tail, the stallion struck the prince's right eye out! Leaving the moaning rider on the ground, the horse spread his mighty wings and flew off.

Dazed with pain, Agib opened his one good eye and recognized the palace where the horse had brought him. It was the same mansion that the ten one-eyed youths occupied. On seeing that their would-be avenger had fallen prey to their own mistake, the callous youths sent him away to become a beggar for the rest of his days. Alas! Such a sad ending to this tale from the Arabian Nights.

From *The Arabian Nights: Their Best-Known Tales*, edited by Kate Douglas Wiggin and Nora A. Smith (Charles Scribner's Sons, 1909).

THE CHIMERA
(FOUNTAINS OF PIRENE)

BY NATHANIEL HAWTHORNE   RETOLD BY ALMA GILBERT

A handsome brave youth named Bellerophon had been sent to Greece by King Iobates in search of the Fountains of Pirene and the fabled winged horse, Pegasus. The Fountains of Pirene had the sweetest tasting waters of all the country. It was rumored that Pegasus flew down occasionally from its home on top of Mount Helicon to taste the sweet rushing waters of Pirene.

Bellerophon had been told by the wise men of his country that he would need the bravery and fleetness of Pegasus in order to reach the heights of the impenetrable mountain where the dreaded monster Chimera lived, terrorizing all nearby towns. Bellerophon was to fight the Chimera and vanquish it so that people could live in peace.

Bellerophon arrived at Pirene with a magic sword, a jeweled bridle, and a golden bit. Two children showed Bellerophon where the horse might alight. Then all three hid near the fountains and waited to catch a glimpse of Pegasus.

After several weeks of waiting, their patience was rewarded. The beautiful winged horse flew down, alighted, and began tasting the sweet, cool waters. Bellerophon saw his chance, and jumping out of his hiding place onto Pegasus's back, he threw the bridle over the majestic head before the startled great horse could react. Rearing up and pawing the air with its hooves, Pegasus tried vainly to throw off the intruder on its back. The winged horse flew up into the clouds rearing and heaving, but Bellerophon managed to stay on. Days later the immortal horse, exhausted from all its efforts, came to rest on a high cumulus cloud and surrendered itself to Bellerophon.

The youth, full of admiration for the courage, beauty, and power of Pegasus, offered the winged horse its freedom. The valiant steed, grateful for this act of kindness, promised to help Bellerophon conquer the Chimera.

Together they flew to the mountain cave where the dreaded fire-breathing monster lived. The mighty horse flew so close to the fiendish Chimera, which spewed fire on all who dared approach, that its beautiful white wings were singed by the fire. Because of Pegasus's bravery, Bellerophon was able to get close enough to cut off the Chimera's head with three strokes of his magic sword.

They flew home together to Bellerophon's home to tell King Iobates that the Chimera had been destroyed. As a reward for its services to Bellerophon, King Iobates set Pegasus free. The mighty horse, after saying good-bye to its friend, flew back to its home on top of Mount Helicon where the sages tell us it still lives to this day.

From *A Wonder-Book for Girls and Boys* (Ticknor, 1852).

SEEIN' THINGS

BY EUGENE FIELD

I ain't afeard uv snakes, or toads, or bugs, or worms, or mice,
An' things 'at girls are skeered uv I think are awful nice!
I'm pretty brave, I guess; an' yet I hate to go to bed,
For when I'm tucked up warm an' snug an' when my prayers are said,
Mother tells me "Happy dreams!" and takes away the light,
An' leaves me lyin' all alone an' seein' things at night!

Sometimes they're in the corner, sometimes they're by the door,
Sometimes they're all a-standin' in the middle uv the floor;
Sometimes they are a-sittin' down, sometimes they're walkin' round
So softly an' so creepylike they never make a sound!
Sometimes they are as black as ink, an' other times they're white—
But the color ain't no difference when you see things at night!

Once, when I licked a feller 'at had just moved on our street,
An' father sent me up to bed without a bite to eat,
I woke up in the dark an' saw things standin' in a row,
A-lookin' at me cross-eyed an' p'intin' at me—so!
Oh, my! I wuz so skeered that time I never slep' a mite—
It's almost alluz when I'm bad I see things at night!

Lucky thing I ain't a girl, or I'd be skeered to death!
Bein' I'm a boy, I duck my head an' hold my breath;
An' I am, oh! *so* sorry I'm a naughty boy, an' then
I promise to be better an' I say my prayers again!
Gran'ma tells me that's the only way to make it right
When a feller has been wicked an' sees things at night!

An' so, when other naughty boys would coax me into sin,
I try to skwush the Tempter's voice 'at urges me within;
An' when they's pie for supper, or cakes 'at's big an' nice,

I want to——but I do not pass my plate f'r them things twice!
No, ruther let Starvation wipe me slowly out o' sight
Than I should keep a-livin' on an' seein' things at night!

SINBAD IN
THE VALLEY OF DIAMONDS

RETOLD BY ALMA GILBERT

O nce upon a time during the reign of the Caliph Haroun al-Raschid, there lived in the city of Bagdad a wealthy merchant named Sinbad the sailor, who had undertaken a series of adventurous voyages during his lifetime. These had earned him not only unrivalled fame but a very large fortune. The following is a tale of one such voyage.

After successfully completing his first major voyage Sinbad had again grown weary of living at home and longed for the adventures of the high seas. He undertook a second voyage with other merchants en route to Persia. When the ship stopped at an island to replenish its provisions, Sinbad was inadvertently left behind. Full of terror and despair upon finding that his ship had left without him, Sinbad walked around aimlessly until he spied a shiny giant egg in the distance. Coming closer, he recognized it as the egg of a large predatory bird called a roc. The bird was so large that its legs were the size of small tree trunks.

Sinbad saw that by tying his turban to the roc's leg, he could leave the deserted island. When the bird flew away, it carried Sinbad clutching the end of his unravelled turban. The roc finally landed, and Sinbad found himself in a valley below a lofty mountain where the ground was strewn with shining pebbles. Sinbad examined them and found the pebbles to be diamonds of varying sizes. He had been dropped in the fabled Valley of Diamonds! The sides of the valley were so steep that it was impossible to ascend its cliffs.

While Sinbad pondered how to leave the valley with as many of its shiny pebbles as he could carry, a vulture alighted and began scratching around looking for trapped carrion to devour. Finding nothing edible other than Sinbad, the bird of prey snatched its intended meal and flew out of the Valley of Diamonds carrying Sinbad.

When the vulture landed, Sinbad escaped its claws and hid in a crevice until the bird grew tired of looking for him. To his surprise, he found another merchant who had been lying in wait for the vulture, hoping to pick off some precious stones that might have adhered to carrion from the Valley of Diamonds.

The merchant was delighted to find that Sinbad had stuffed his pockets with the diamonds. The two found their way to the harbor where luckily Sinbad's own ship was moored and taking on provisions. After Sinbad had identified himself and the luggage he'd left aboard, the two plucky merchants caught a ride home to Bagdad with goods, diamonds, and lives intact. So ended the second voyage of Sinbad the sailor.

From *The Arabian Nights: Their Best-Known Tales*, edited by Kate Douglas Wiggin and Nora A. Smith (Charles Scribner's Sons, 1909).

JACK AND THE BEANSTALK

TRADITIONAL ENGLISH FOLKTALE   RETOLD BY ALMA GILBERT

Once upon a time in a far, far away country there lived a poor widow with her only son, Jack. Because they were in great need of food and supplies, the widow sent Jack out with their one possession, a milking cow named Bessie, to be sold for a few pieces of gold. On his way to market, Jack found a stranger who offered him some magical beans for the cow, promising that they would make him rich.

His mother was not happy at all with the trade. Disconsolate, she threw the magic beans out the window and sent Jack to bed without his supper. The next morning, to everyone's surprise the little beans had grown into a huge vine, which climbed and climbed, losing itself up in the clouds. Jack decided to see where the vine ended. He still believed that those magic beans would lead to his fame and fortune.

Up, up he climbed, past the clouds into a wonderful land where in the distance, a marvelous castle stood shimmering in the early morning light. What must have been Jack's surprise when he discovered that the castle belonged to a man-eating giant?

The giant's wife felt sorry for the boy and hid him from her husband.

"Fee, fie, fo, fum! I smell the blood of an Englishman!" cried the giant upon entering the room.

"Nonsense, man!" replied his wife. "Here. Sit down and have your breakfast."

Safely tucked away in the flour barrel, Jack spied the giant playing with some of his treasures: a hen that laid golden eggs and a singing harp. "So that's my fame and fortune," thought Jack from the flour barrel. "Let's see if I can lift them from this man-eating giant."

After playing with his hen and harp, the giant finally dozed off. Quickly, Jack sprang out from the barrel, snatched the hen and harp, and began running as fast as his legs would carry him. He did not count on the harp's giving him away, but she did.

"Help, Master! Help! I'm being abducted," cried the singing harp. Her cries awakened the giant, who began a hot pursuit of the boy already scampering down the giant vine.

"Mother dearest! Mother dearest!" shouted Jack as he clambered down. "Quick! Fetch the ax and cut down the vine!" His mother heard the voice of her son coming from somewhere up in the vine, so she quickly fetched the ax and began chopping away at the giant vine.

Within a few minutes, Jack made it to the bottom and taking the ax from his mother applied the last blows which brought down the huge vine and the giant with it. The happy part of the story is that with the golden eggs and singing harp, Jack and his mother lived comfortably and happily ever after.

THE HISTORY OF CODADAD AND HIS BROTHERS

RETOLD BY ALMA GILBERT

T he great sultan of Harran had fifty sons all of whom he loved but Codadad. The sultan had conceived such an aversion to the poor youth that he sent him along with his mother, Priouzè, to be brought up at the distant court of the king of Samaria.

That ruler spared no pains in training the youngster, and at eighteen he was looked upon as a prodigy. Wishing to get back into his own father's good graces, Codadad resolved to enter his service in disguise, fight his enemies, and win his father's esteem before revealing his identity.

He succeeded so well that his father made him governor of the other princes, his brothers. These young men so resented the stranger's advancement that they plotted to ruin him. They asked for his permission to go hunting and then disappeared. When they did not return after three days, the sultan blamed Codadad for their loss and ordered him to find them or lose his life.

After searching for some days, the prince came to a palace of black marble. At one of the windows was a beautiful lady named Deryabar who warned him to make his escape because the master of the castle was a ferocious giant who lived on human flesh. No sooner had she spoken, than the giant appeared. With the help of Allah and his trusty sword, Codadad killed the giant and released all of the prisoners, including his faithless brothers whom the giant had also captured and the beautiful princess Deryabar.

Deryabar told Codadad that she was a sultan's daughter. Her father had been murdered, but she had escaped with the help of the grand vizier. She had married a young sultan, but had again met with misfortune. Their ship had been captured by a band of pirates. A beautiful vessel had approached them and the sultan and his young wife, thinking it was a merchant ship, had allowed the occupants to come aboard. Instead of kindly merchants offering their wares, armed pirates boarded the sultan's ship, slew him, and captured Deryabar.

Codadad revealed his identity to his brothers and invited them to witness his betrothal to the beautiful Deryabar. In jealousy they stabbed him and left him for dead. Codadad recovered and rescued his ungrateful brothers from a band of pirates who had advanced against his father, the Sultan.

Harran, grateful and contrite for the ill treatment he had given his youngest son, restored to Codadad all the honors that belonged to him, including marriage to the beautiful

Deryabar who had come to tell Harran of the cowardice and weakness of the other brothers and ask for justice. The magnanimous Codadad prevailed upon his father not to put his wicked brothers to death. They were banished from the court instead, but allowed to stay in the kingdom to serve Codadad and his bride. Codadad became the sole heir to the kingdom and he and Deryabar ruled well, attended by the brothers who finally saw the error of their wicked ways and served their good brother during their entire lives.

From *The Arabian Nights: Their Best-Known Tales*, edited by Kate Douglas Wiggin and Nora A. Smith (Charles Scribner's Sons, 1909).

SING A SONG O' SIXPENCE

TRADITIONAL MOTHER GOOSE RHYME

Sing a song o' sixpence,
A pocket full of rye,
Four-and-twenty blackbirds
Baked in a pie.
When the pie was opened,
The birds began to sing;
Wasn't that a dainty dish to set before a king?

CIRCE'S PALACE

BY NATHANIEL HAWTHORNE   RETOLD BY ALMA GILBERT

King Ulysses and his men, after the long siege of the battle of Troy, were returning home when a hurricane threw them off course. The storm finally tossed their ship into the cove of a beautiful green island where they sought shelter until the winds abated. Ulysses and a party of his men explored the island for food and water, which they had lost during the storm.

The party of sailors led by King Ulysses spied the marble towers of a palace rising on the crest of a hill. They trudged uphill until they came closer and could smell the succulent aromas of baking bread. Ulysses entered the palace gardens where he was confronted by a tiny bird, beating its wings furiously as if to warn him of a nearby danger.

Ulysses and his men heeded the bird's warning. They cast lots to see who was to continue, and Eurylochus, one of his lieutenants, was chosen to survey the area with a smaller party.

The hungry sailors were met first by a pack of lions, tigers, and wolves, which instead of attacking them, seemed to want to cajole them inside. Eurylochus suggested caution, but the weary soldiers followed their stomachs to where the wonderful smells of baking bread lured them. The party was met at the palace steps by Queen Circe, a beautiful enchantress who waved a magic wand and turned all the sailors into swine. "Gluttonous men, you have now taken the forms of the beasts you most resemble!" thundered Circe. "Lead them away to be fed, fattened, and later butchered!"

Eurylochus, who had not succumbed to his men's appetites and had stayed behind, witnessed the entire sight. He raced back to Ulysses and they formed a plan to rescue their men. Zeus, king of the gods, decided to help good King Ulysses. He sent Mercury with instructions to Ulysses not to eat or drink anything Circe might hand him.

Ulysses confronted Circe but would not touch any of the proffered food or drink. Instead, unsheathing his sword, he threatened the enchantress with instant death unless Circe returned his sailors to their human forms. Seeing that her powers were of no avail, for Ulysses was protected by Zeus, Mercury, and his own good works, Circe relented. Waving her magic wand, she restored to human form all of the sailors.

Ulysses asked her to also free the little bird that had initially warned them. Circe obliged. The bird took as its human form that of King Picus, who because of his arrogance had been turned into a tiny prancing bird. Picus thanked Ulysses profusely and promised to become the lifelong servant of his people, seeing to it that they prospered instead of profiting himself from their toil.

Ulysses, Eurylochus, and their men hurried off the island, leaving Circe to trap the souls of men whose conduct on earth did not make them worthy of human form.

From *Tanglewood Tales for Girls and Boys; being a second Wonder-Book* (Ticknor, 1853).

THE RELUCTANT DRAGON

BY KENNETH GRAHAME   RETOLD BY ALMA GILBERT

Along time ago in a nearby cottage halfway between a village and the next, there lived a very bright young chap, the son of the local shepherd, who read every book that he could lay his hands on when he wasn't helping his father with the flocks.

One day, the shepherd announced that he had seen what appeared to him like a dragon in a nearby cave. Why, of course Boy had to investigate. The boy assured his father that dragons should not be bothered because usually they were sensitive creatures that needed special handling or else they'd go off something fierce!

The next morning Boy strolled over and sure enough! He found a rather large dragon stretched lazily in the sun purring with regularity. It was soon evident that this dragon was not your usual sort. Certainly not like his fellow dragons at all, spewing fire and going about harassing the neighbors. This dragon was a Philosopher. He read poetry and like to sit around and just *think*.

The boy and the dragon soon became fast friends. Boy could always be relied upon to listen politely to the dragon's latest composition. Unfortunately rumors of his presence made the villagers edgy and they persuaded St. George, the local saint and dragon fighter, to rid them of their scourge.

When Boy heard of this, he tried to dissuade St. George from dispatching his dragon. Of course the dragon was not one bit interested in fighting and could not be prevailed upon to even put up a show of courage. After much back and forth discussion, St. George met the dragon and ascertained that yes, indeed, this was a polite type of Beast not at all interested in damaging the locals or polluting the environment. It was decided that perhaps just a "pretend" type of battle could be staged for local consumption.

The dragon did not disappoint his admirers. He was such a *ham*! He showed up the next day on the jousting field, his scales polished to a high gloss and breathing the obligatory puffs of fire.

St. George winked at Boy and the dragon and then with a great show of clamor and clank of armor, he charged the ferocious-appearing beast. The dragon put on a great show, stomping, pawing the ground, and beating his great tail in defiance. He even managed, in one of the knight's passes, to singe the plumes of his helmet with a fiery roar. The time came, however, for the Saint to polish off the Beast who was making a better impression on the villagers than he was.

Again the combatants faced each other one last time. The end was quick. All that the boy and villagers saw was the lightning movement of the Saint's arm as he threw his lance. When the dust settled, there stood the Saint over the Beast's inert body. The boy's heart stood still! What had gone wrong? Nobody was supposed to get hurt! Certainly not his gentle Dragon! Had his poor friend, reluctant to the end to engage in any form of hooliganism, been mortally wounded after all?

Not so! Not so! As Boy approached, Dragon opened one eye and winked conspiratorially. The wily beast was simply holding the lance between his body and arm and just simply playing possum! The Saint assured the villagers that the dragon had been tamed and had certainly learned his lesson. He extracted from the dragon a solemn promise never, *never* to disturb or be a nuisance to the quiet community. This done, Boy, Saint, Dragon, and villagers repaired to the village to sing and celebrate this jolly event. One couldn't be certain who was doing the loudest singing, but the consensus was that it must have been the dragon.

From *Dream Days* (London: John Lane: The Bodley Head, 1898; with Maxfield Parrish's illustrations, 1902).

AUTHOR'S NOTE

"There was a place in childhood that I remember well, and
there is a voice of sweetest tone, bright fairy tales did tell …"
—from *My Mother Dear*, Samuel Lover (1797–1868)

My interest in the life and art of Maxfield Parrish can be traced to early childhood and to a passion for beautifully illustrated books of fairy tales. These marvelous stories were first read to me by my mother and godmother and were later given to me as gifts when I was old enough to begin reading myself.

I was an only child raised in a literate, old-fashioned family of the Mexican aristocracy at a time of great economic and political upheaval. During this confusing and often frightening period, my family was understandably protective. I was seldom allowed to go out or to invite other children to our home to play with me. Frequently left alone with only books for company, I became a tireless and voracious reader.

There was a special spot in our house that I dearly loved and claimed as my own secret reading place. Our living room had large French doors draped in heavy damask and velvet curtains leading to a wrought-iron balcony overlooking the streets below. I sat for hours unnoticed in the space between the curtain and the balcony, a favorite book of fairy tales or a lavishly illustrated adventure book propped before me on my lap.

Alma Gilbert at the age of three.

As I grew older, my library expanded to include illustrated editions of *The Adventures of Tom Sawyer* and *The Adventures of Huckleberry Finn*, as well as the swashbuckling stories of *King Arthur*, *Ivanhoe*, *The Last of the Mohicans*, and others. These books introduced me to the great nineteenth-century American illustrators Howard Pyle and N. C. Wyeth.

It was my first copy of *The Arabian Nights*, purchased by a favorite aunt when I was ten, in which I encountered the heart-stoppingly beautiful paintings by Maxfield Parrish. Little did I know then that this was the book that would inspire my life-long involvement with his work.

After attending university, I married in 1959 and, because of my own solitary childhood, longed for a large family. I adopted eight children and once again my cherished collection of children's books became part of a beloved ritual in my life. It was my turn to read to my own children, to guide their little fingers over the words and watch their rapt faces as the stories unfolded.

By 1973 I was a successful art dealer in Northern California. One fateful day a client asked if I could find a Maxfield Parrish oil for him. Until then, it had never occurred to me that one could actually *own* the astonishing illustrations I had loved as a child and, quite literally, grown up with. I began a nine-month search which culminated in my finding not one but twenty-three paintings at the Vose Galleries of Boston. I shall never forget walking into that room—a room filled with the magical images of my childhood. There they stood, stacked one in front of another. I felt like Ali Baba himself stumbling into the treasure cave for the first time. I made a choice right then and there that irrevocably changed the course of my life. I decided to mortgage my house and purchase seventeen of the twenty-three paintings. Predictably, the Parrish exhibition held from that acquisition was a resounding success! All seventeen works sold within a month.

Five years later, buoyed by the continuing interest that my Parrish exhibits were enjoying across the country, I took another fateful step. I sold my home in California and purchased "The Oaks," the house that Parrish had built in Cornish, New Hampshire, and where he lived and worked most of his life. In June of 1978, I made another dream come true and the Parrish Museum opened its doors to the world.

My happiest memories of those times are of sitting before the immense stone fireplace in the music room with my children gathered around me. I shall always remember the warmth and crackle of the fire and the quiet benediction of the swirling snow outside as I read our favorite stories aloud.

After seven years and with much regret, I gave up the maintenance of "The Oaks." The financial and emotional hardships of trying to direct a nonprofit museum and run a flourishing gallery on opposite sides of the country finally took their toll and I returned to California.

Since those uncertain days, it has been my good fortune to have seen and even held many of the paintings presented in this book. And it has been my mission and my great pleasure to help revive and maintain interest in one of the true giants of American painting. Parrish's contribution to the worlds of art *and* literature is, perhaps, unique in history. As I grow older, I keep my mind and spirit young by surrounding myself with these glorious images that were such an important part of my youth and continue to play a vital role in my life today.

It is to all children and to all those who are children at heart that I dedicate this book. May you all find within these pages the enjoyment that one little girl did many, many years ago in another place, in another time.

NOTES ON THE ILLUSTRATIONS

ILLUSTRATION SOURCES

NOTES ON THE ILLUSTRATIONS

I n 1894, American poet Eugene Field published the last of five books of sentimental poems for and about children. The final volume, originally entitled *Love Songs of Childhood*, was published by Charles Scribner's Sons in 1905 under the title *Poems of Childhood*. Edward Bok, the editor of *Ladies' Home Journal*, commissioned Parrish to illustrate five of the Field poems for his magazine. When Charles Scribner heard about the illustrations, he asked Parrish for a cover design, endpapers, and a title page, in addition to the five paintings for his new edition. (Parrish misspelled his own name on the title page. No one caught it, not even sharp-eyed Parrish himself.) *Poems of Childhood* was the first book in which Parrish's paintings were reproduced in full-color. It is the best known of all books illustrated by him, largely due to *The Dinkey-Bird* (page 27), which is perhaps his most recognizable image. Other illustrations from *Poems of Childhood* in this book are *The Sugar-Plum Tree* (page 32), *Wynken, Blynken, and Nod* (page 36), *With Trumpet and Drum* (page 45), *The Fly-Away Horse* (page 54), and *Seein' Things* (page 61).

Themes and images from childhood are favorite motifs in Parrish's repertoire and he used them in unexpected and innovative ways. *Old King Cole* (page 13), *Sing a Song o' Sixpence* (page 69), and *The Pied Piper* (page 20) were all done originally as murals.

In 1915 Parrish received a commission from the D. M. Ferry Seed Company for a series of posters: *Peter, Peter, Pumpkin Eater* (page 31), *Peter Piper* (page 3), *Mary, Mary, Quite Contrary* (page 50), and *Jack and the Beanstalk* (page 64). The over-sized figures and scaled-down backgrounds, unmarred by logo or ad copy, were startlingly avant-garde according to the advertising standards of the day.

In 1912 Parrish planned a series of paintings based on the general theme of "Once upon a time...." His friend Will Bradley, the art editor for William Randolph Hearst's *Good Housekeeping*, asked him to do the series for his magazine before offering them to any other publishers. Parrish agreed to illustrate twelve fairy tales over a period of two years. *Good Housekeeping* commissioned the reproduction rights of each painting, with the understanding that the original works would be returned to the artist.

No one had counted on the iron will of William Randolph Hearst. When the first three paintings, including *The Frog Prince* (page 14) and *Snow White and the Seven Dwarfs* (page 39) (originally called *Snow Drop* from the old, no longer used title of the tale, *The Story of Snow Drop*), appeared in Bradley's office, Hearst was so taken by the workmanship and artistry that he pulled them away from *Good Housekeeping* and used them for the covers of *Hearst's* for the

June, July, and August issues. He told Parrish that he liked them so well that he wanted to own the series outright. Parrish was somewhat taken aback since he had planned to use the pictures himself in a collection of fairy tales. Disappointed that he would not be working with his friend Will Bradley, Parrish did not deliver the next painting, *Sleeping Beauty*, until November of that year. *Cinderella* (page 24) was not completed until March 1914. Hearst used it as a cover for *Harper's Bazaar*. The last painting Parrish did for a Hearst publication was *Puss-in-Boots* (page 53). It appeared on the cover of *Hearst's* in May 1914. Hearst admired it so much that he kept it. Parrish did not take kindly to this cavalier attitude and never fulfilled the original commission.

This group of paintings illustrates the tremendous range of style and mood Parrish had at his command. The dreamy elegance of *Cinderella* is a lyric contrast to the brooding pathos of *Snow White* and the witty charm of *Puss-in-Boots*.

Not long after completing *The House of Seven Gables*, Nathaniel Hawthorne (1804–1864) sketched out his plan for *A Wonder-Book and Tanglewood Tales* in a letter to his friend James T. Fields. "I mean to write within six weeks or two months a book of stories made up of classical myths. The subjects are: The Story of Midas with the Golden Touch, Pandora's Box, The Adventures of Atlas, Bellerophon, and Jason and His Teacher. These, I think, will be enough to make up a volume. As a framework, I shall have a young college student telling these stories to his cousins, brothers, and sisters during their vacations, sometimes in the woods and dells. Unless I greatly mistake, these old fictions will work admirably for the purpose; I shall aim in substituting a tone in some degree Gothic or romantic; or any such tones as may best please myself instead of the classic coldness, which is as repellent as the touch of marble." [1]

The manuscript of *A Wonder-Book and Tanglewood Tales* is the only one of Hawthorne's works to have survived in its original state and is still owned by one of his descendants. It was written on thin blue paper on both sides of the page with very few erasures or corrections. The work was originally illustrated with etchings and was issued in two volumes: *A Wonder-Book for Girls and Boys* (1852) and *Tanglewood Tales for Girls and Boys; being a second Wonder-Book* (1853). It was a huge success. Duffield and Company published it in a single volume in 1910 with illustrations by Maxfield Parrish. This edition was even more popular than the earlier printings.

The paintings for *A Wonder-Book and Tanglewood Tales* were commissioned from the artist by *Collier's*. They were large oils on canvas laid down on board. Some, like *The Chimera* (page 58), had a chiaroscuro that was difficult to reproduce in a magazine, but they were beautifully executed in the Duffield and Company edition. In *Cadmus Sowing the Dragon's Teeth* (page 35) the viewer finds a stunning example of Parrish's use of heroic drapery billowing magnificiently around his figure, dramatically highlighted against brilliantly hued landscapes. The unusual scale and perspective of the figures to the settings creates a surreal, otherworldly quality to this group of paintings, not seen before in children's book illustration.

[1] © Nathaniel Hawthorne, from letter to James T. Fields, May 2, 1851. "Introductory Notes" by George Parsons Lathrop, *A Wonder-Book for Girls and Boys* (Boston and New York: Houghton Mifflin and Company, 1887; Riverside Edition, Volume IV).

The historical origins of the collection of stories we know today as "The Arabian Nights" remain as mysterious and exotic as the stories themselves. Since at least the Middle Ages they have been preserved and handed down from generation to generation thanks to the rich oral tradition of Arab storytellers. Over time the tales may have gradually found a framework in the story of the jealous King Schahriah who took a new wife each night and had her put to death each morning. That is until the lovely Scheherazade won a reprieve for a thousand and one nights by fascinating the king each evening with a story.

By the fifteenth century the stories began to appear in written form. Since that time they have been translated into dozens of languages. For the last century, Edward Williams Lane's version has been accepted as the standard English translation. In 1909 Charles Scribner's Sons published an edition of *The Arabian Nights: Their Best-Known Tales* edited for juvenile readers by Nora A. Smith and Kate Douglas Wiggin with illustrations by Maxfield Parrish.

The exotic settings of *The Arabian Nights* gave Parrish perhaps his most dramatic showcase for not only his magnificent sense of color and unmatched handling of light, but also for his extensive architectural training. The over-scaled urns, cascading flights of steps, serene reflecting pools, and immense flowering shrubs that adorned his home and gardens at "The Oaks" appear again and again in this series of paintings. His use of brilliant, jewel-like hues in *Codadad* (page 67) and the magical treatment of light in *Prince Agib* (page 57) offer eloquent testimony to Parrish's unique contribution to American art and literature.

Following their success with *The Golden Age* (1899), Kenneth Grahame, beloved author of *The Wind in the Willows*, and Maxfield Parrish were reunited for a second collaboration. Parrish was commissioned to do ten full-color paintings for the companion volume, *Dream Days* (1902), in contrast to the exclusively monochrome illustrations he had created for the earlier book. Because of technical difficulties with color lithography at the turn of the century, the paintings for *Dream Days* were reproduced in black-and-white after all, using a then new photogravure process. Two of the paintings, *The Reluctant Dragon* (page 72) and *Dies Irae* (page 2), are reproduced here in their original glorious color, just as Parrish intended.

ILLUSTRATION SOURCES

The author and publisher gratefully acknowledge the following sources for permission to reproduce the illustrations on the pages listed below.

page 2   *Dies Irae*, 1902. Color lithograph. Collection of the author.

page 3   *Peter Piper*, 1919. Oil on board. 29 5/8 x 22 ins. Department of Special Collections, University of California Library, Davis, Calif. Collection of the Ferry-Morse Seed Company Archives.

page 13   *Old King Cole*, 1897. Triptych. Ink, watercolor, and gouache on paper. (A) 14 x 9 ins. (B) 14 x 17 ins. (C) 14 x 9 ins. Collection of the Pennsylvania Academy of the Fine Arts, Philadelphia. Henry D. Gilpin Fund.

page 14   *The Frog Prince*, 1912. Color lithograph. Collection of the author.

page 17   *The Golden Fleece* (The Argonauts in Quest of the Golden Fleece), 1909. Color lithograph. Collection of the author.

pages 20–21   *The Pied Pier of Hamelin*, 1909. Oil on canvas laid down on board. 7 x 16 ft. Collection Sheraton Palace Hotel, San Francisco, Calif. Photograph courtesy of the Sheraton Palace Hotel.

page 23   *Humpty Dumpty*, 1897. Pen and ink. 16 3/4 x 12 ins. Syracuse University Art Collection, Syracuse, N.Y.

page 24   *Cinderella (Enchantment)*, 1914. Oil on board. 32 x 26 ins. Private collection.

page 27   *The Dinkey-Bird*, 1904. Oil on paper. 21 1/2 x 15 1/2 ins. Collection of the Charles Hosmer Morse Museum of American Art, Winter Park, Fla.

page 28   *The Story of Aladdin (Aladdin and the African Magician)*, 1905. Oil on glazed paper. 18 x 16 ins. Collection of the Detroit Institute of Arts, Detroit, Mich. Bequest of Mr. and Mrs. Lawrence P. Fisher.

page 31 and jacket (inset)   *Peter, Peter, Pumpkin-Eater*, 1918. Oil on board. 31 x 23 7/8 ins. Department of Special Collections, University of California Library, Davis, Calif. Collection of the Ferry-Morse Seed Company Archives.

INDEX

Note: Page numbers in **bold** type indicate illustrations.